AF360217

Call Him by Any Name

Chandu or Chand or Chander

JMLK

Inkfeathers Publishing

www.inkfeathers.com

Call Him By Any Name
Written by Jag Mohan Lal Khurana
Paperback Edition

First Published in India in 2022
by Inkfeathers Publishing, New Delhi 110095

Copyright © Jag Mohan Lal Khurana 2022
Cover Design © Jag Mohan Lal Khurana 2022
Cover Image © Twenty20.com

All rights reserved.

ISBN 978-93-90882-55-7

Without limiting the rights under copyright reserved above, no
part of this publication may be reproduced, lent, resold, or
transmitted by any means, electronic, mechanical, photocopying
or otherwise, without the prior permission of both the copyright
owner and the publisher of this book.

www.inkfeathers.com

Contents

Preface

The author has in this book brought out the fact that one's own frame of mind and attitude matters a lot in one's own development. Any situation that one may find oneself in, whether by choice or by imposition, is by and large man made and therefore has a solution. To view it in a certain light is to see the silver lining behind every dark cloud. It is the authors endeavour to help see the true reality of things, as Chander does in the various situations as and when they arise.

The author calls his book, 'Call Him By Any Name- Chandu, Chand or Chander'. This is borrowed from the well-known saying in Hindi, 'Maya ke hain teen naam, Parsu, Parsa, Parsram'. Chander's environ changes frequently and he finds himself to be seen as Chandu or Chand or Chander depending on where he is and the standing he has in the given situation.

The motivation to author this book came at Dharamshala. The author had been closely associated with Tushita in Delhi and had gone to His Holiness the Venerable Dalai Lama to attend a discourse. During his stay, he felt like sharing his experiences in the light of his teachings.

Since it had been on my mind for many years, it took just a few weeks to write the first manuscript.

It is common to hear, "One must always be positive or have a positive mental attitude." What is this positive frame of mind ? How do we go about having it ? Is there a push button that the present day technology can give us. Have they not yet developed a gadget or gizmo that can be clipped or worn on your wrist and thereafter everything will be hunky-dory. W. Clemenstone's book, 'How to Develop a Positive Mental Attitude' is one of the best books that gives us a way to get started.

Training of mind has already been introduced at high school level in many countries. The students learn to achieve peace of mind by practising various techniques. Whether we are conscious of it or not, we are interdependent and inter-connected. Our behaviour effects not only us but also others around us. How we perceive events, and our attitude effects everyone else though to a varying degree? We may choose to have our own utopia, rejecting all or accepting all religions. But to the society we live in, it should be acceptable. What is acceptable depends on the liberal or conservative norms of the group you belong to. In the present day we see an increasing tolerance in our multi caste, multiracial and secular groupings. While accepting one's own religion to be a matter of personal choice, a pragmatic approach would be, as Dr. Karan Singh counsels, to look for that golden thread that runs through all religions and social beliefs, and lay the stress on that commonality, to seek, the universal message of love. Love always triumphs.

There is always room for improvement. We have to find a better way of doing things. So we tell ourselves when it comes to improving things in the work environment. How about starting on another journey?

This journey that we shall be talking about is a personal journey. Of course there is a well-defined goal - a goal that we have set for ourself. The trick lies in the breaking of the goal to mini goals. The time we give ourselves to achieve these mini goal, is a matter of limited importance. In self-development one need not rush nor does the time we allot to ourself to achieve the mini goal should be of much importance. It is for one's own satisfaction and move on to the next mini goal. The emerging confidence in oneself on achieving the mini goal is of essence. Time taken is of little consideration. Do not forget it depends on at what level you are today and to what level you want to get at.

Our thinking pattern is a sum total of our childhood habits, childlike ways to get what we want, conditioned responses, cliches, our pleasant and unpleasant experiences and so on and so fore. A time comes in everyone's life when you want to examine your own life. It is an examined and a way of life of our own choosing that we want to live. Human beings are gifted with a mind, and we should take a full advantage of that to make our own decisions.

To overcome our delusions, we have to forget the various coloured glasses we are accustomed to. It is these colours of the glasses we see through that are the cause of our stereotyped responses in most of the situations. One has to begin by overcoming the delusions and understand the true reality of things. This is the new journey. Knowing the cause of the delusions is learning how to overcome. A realisation of the impermanence of any phenomenon in the light of dependent origination and it's emptiness shall lead you to a new way of looking at things and you shall overcome. It may seem difficult to understand at first because it is abstract. Contemplation and meditation makes it easier to comprehend. The existence of phenomenon is accepted but its independent existence is denied. There is cause and effect. The causality has to be understood. At times we see darkness all around us. Dark clouds do appear. So dark they are that day begins to appear as night. They clouds thunder. Sometimes there is lightning. Then the cloud bursts. There is a thunderstorm, and it pours. After some time the rain stops, and it is all over. Samsara is over. Day light appears again. The sun comes out and it is all clear. You may see the rainbow. Here the causality is that water vapours turn into liquid droplets. Moist air rises upward and becomes colder. The air cannot hold all the water vapour in it. So some water vapour condenses to form water droplets. As the droplets grow bigger and bigger and when the drops become heavy they fall to the ground, and we have rain. The cause and effect is very clear. Furthermore there is nothing permanent. After the rain there are no clouds. Likewise, a student may be very uptight about forthcoming exams but depending on his preparation he will perform. When the exams are over there is no worry or no cause to be uptight.

As you go along, bit by bit, you shall shed your old beliefs and habits to become a new person. The positive frame of mind will now be a way of life; indeed you shall live it. As Krishna tells Arjuna, "I cannot traverse the path till I become the path, I am the path." So you be a Positive Thinking Man. You shall make giant strides and reach new heights that had hitherto been beyond your imagination.

The Motivation to the Author

One last point before I wish you a happy journey. It is human nature to regress and fall back to old negative ways. It's like getting back to square one. Do not be disheartened. Don't allow despair to creep in. Even monks, priests and all spiritual people know this problem. For them it ceases to be a problem because they are aware of it and have developed mechanism to get over it. Even His Holiness Shankaracharyaji also goes to Joshi Math after he helps convicts, thieves, and skid row men. Whether they do tapas or meditation in their aloofness- call it by any name, all the same they have to get their bearings back or let's say reinforce their convictions, their beliefs and indeed their mission in life, from time to time. You Mr. Positive Man who is going out everyday mixing and interacting in a world abounding in negative and manipulative people, have to take it in stride. Self-actualised people are hard to find. Whether you choose to pray or meditate or seek inspiration in nature (mountains or ashram or special places abounding in greenery) you will have to find some way to revitalise and reinvigorate yourself. In only a few cases a change of location may be desirable and recommendable.

Chapter I

Childhood

Years 1947 to 1959

Chander was born at a time when the subcontinent of India was having joy, happiness, and celebrations. India had gained freedom from the British yoke. Indeed the event was perceived as beacon for the Asian and African countries who still suffered under colonialism. India had become a symbol of Mahatma Gandhi's nonviolence and Jawaharlal Nehru's peaceful coexistence. India had woken up to a tryst with destiny determined to usher in an era of a socialist society. Pakistan had joined the community of nations. It was 1947.

Unfortunately such a large accomplishment was marred by a partition of the subcontinent, resulting in an unpredictably large movement of the population across the new borders of the two countries. Millions of Muslims left India to migrate to Pakistan and millions of Hindus, Sikhs and Bengalis left Pakistan migrating to India. That was not enough. As the genocidal transfer of population was going on, fundamentalist and misguided people had their way. Murders, riots, looting and kidnapping of children had become rampant. There was hardly any family in Punjab and Bengal, on both sides of the border, which was not grief stricken. So deep were the wounds that even today, more than two and a half generations the scars are still there. May be in another decade or two, the process of reconciliation and healing can begin. The cause exists and the dream will not be denied. The positive people will continue to strive till its realisation.

A few hours after Chand's birth, the bags having been already packed, his folks left the house for the railway station. Before leaving they untied the rope round the neck of the cow in the house. The cows face showed she was being left while everyone was leaving. The trains had no timing. When the train to India arrived, they boarded and said goodbye to their home. Uncertainty was there but safety and the collective decision of their community had taken precedence over all other considerations.

Once in India, practically everyone was on his own. To find a village, town or city that would accept the refugees was difficult. In Indian Punjab, though a large number of Muslims had abandoned their houses, the Hindus, by and large, were not allowed to move in. These properties were for the Sikhs. A new scheme of things was being instituted. So they were told. Word got around. Proceed to Delhi. Delhi was the least liked but the only choice.

In Delhi, the camps for the refugees were already overcrowded. They would not take any more refugees. Left with no choice but to look towards relatives who had quarters or houses (mostly those who were living on this side of the border pre partition), many found shelter. Many still were left to strain what they had brought along hoping to find some suitable employment.

The benevolent government of Nehru-Nehru Chacha as children would   look towards him, and Sardar Patel's administrative swiftness, started allotting land for houses to the refugees. Delhi was sparsely populated then, and vast tracks of government land were vacant. The government set up refugee colonies. In those days, typical Punjab culture prevailed. New residents built a room or two at a time. Soon domestic water supply connections were available. Drains were open. With the flush system, drains went underground. All this was accomplished in five years or so since the inception of the Indian Republic. An extraordinary achievement then. Soon the rapid pace with which the Capital city grew was astounding. The sociologist and historians can better answer the motivation and drive that changed the picture so swiftly.

Chand was now proud of his shelter. He could breathe easy and relax. For some years as a child he would not venture out unless he was with an elder or it was something important. This was in contrast to his having been running around and discovering the streets and shops in every neighbourhood that he spent a few months or sometimes nearly a year. With no permanent shelter he could wander off anywhere, sometime for days, much to the chagrin of his parents. At eight he started playing truant. He would sneak out of school at lunch break or sometime join his class at lunch time. He would take long walks in the neighbourhood and decoded the layout and numbering of houses. The engineers had followed a pattern and the numbering, he was told, was based on scriptures. Any good Mahabharata would list the details. Joining groups of boys playing marbles or Guli Danda was more fun. There was something unique about his gait. He would walk, with his head held high, chest out, back straight in a martial manner. This was not in consonance with his father's banking background. It seemed to be more like his own evolution, displayed physically.

Chand's friends would come to see him in the evening. Except for a few, he would hardly ever call on them. Going to the market and park was a standard ritual. Then spending the later part of evening in the local temple for discourse or screening of a movie based on Hindu mythology was part of the routine. This is how were spent the so-called formative years of childhood of Chander.

His playing truant caused a big problem. The neighbours started recognising him and complained to his parents. Many times his aunt, living with them, would come following him. He began to be caught and had to go back to school immediately. So Chand started finding haven in neighbouring colonies and made fantastic friends. It did not last long. Chand had to change his school. He was sent to a distant school, not in the neighbourhood. School bus would take him to school and drop him home in the late afternoon. Most of the students in his new school commuted. He made new friends and started enjoying his studies. His good grades gave a sense of satisfaction to his folks. To him it was like going to a big league from the small league of his local school.

A significant change had come about in Chand. From an outgoing go getter who enjoyed with his schoolmates and classmates, going to market or park to see them did not interest him anymore. All the guys and girls from his local school or neighbourhood had become friends of past. Now he did not want to mix with them. No longer did he get his kicks in fooling around with them. To him knowledge of the subject interested him. Whether it was rules of grammar or facts of history or concept of longitude and latitude they seemed to occupy his mind. When he found himself looking for Los Angeles in South East Asia or was it in Europe in the map of the world, he was driven to familiarise himself with the location of all major cities of the world. He spent many hours with the atlas to know more about nations, their capitals, their currency, their flag and so fore. Then he began to take interest in learning about India's heritage, its historical sites, the empires dating back to Harappan civilisation and how the Bronze Age collapsed. He clearly saw that whether it was Mesopotamia or Mohenjo-Daro, on a macro scale, indeed the world was one. The significant events at a global level - like the fall of Constantinople or destruction of the Spanish Armada etc. and at the local Indian level like the Battle of Plassey, the emergence of the British India Company over the French, the Mutiny or rechristened as First War of Independence in 1857 etc were on his fingertips. The causes of failure in 1857 were of more interest than loafing around. Indeed a slight change of school had played a havoc. It was a change of many seemingly independent factors that had affected a new arising dependent on causes. These causes had no independent existence and the new outlook that had been forged was of dependent origination.

Chapter II

Schooling

Years 1960 to 1964

A consistently good academic performance at school, convinced his parents that he should go to a school with good facilities for science subjects. Then Chand could go to an engineering college. So a school not too distant from home and one that had its students excel in Higher Secondary Board examination was selected. Fortunately, he got admission in the school and Chand began to go to his new school on his bike. Once again, a new environment and new friends was to cause its effect on Chand. Chand found his classmates very studious and reserved with him. They remained so with him for the next three years that he attended the school. His own desire to concentrate on his studies and relate to his classmates only through the studies resulted in his not having any friends. It was more than a year when the tenth class had begun that some guys reached out to him. There was no student in his class from his neighbourhood. It was from adjoining neighbourhoods that he made some acquaintances.

These acquaintances were to become his friends till even more than half a century later.

This school's atmosphere was a little different. The school would plan your whole life including your educational, vocational, and social life. It was at this time that the students went into science or arts stream. The science studying students were further divided into medical or non-medical streams. Those in medical stream had to study biology also. While the lives of all his classmates were being planned, Chandu found himself left out. He had to wait outside his classroom because he was of foreign birth. This was the first time he found himself discriminated. Indeed it was a rude shock to him. Never had he thought that he was different. He was of foreign birth or as was said, "Not India born". Hitherto he had believed that a Hindu born in what was formerly British India and migrated before the adoption of constitution of India whence it became Republic of India on 26th of January 1950, was a full-fledged Indian national in all respects. Apparently it was not so. His interpretation was now corrected. All laws do not have to be accepted to the letter. The spirit was different. While studying in the eleventh class, he had been convinced that he did not have a right to education in free India. It was the large heartedness of the Indian people that he was in school. One eligible Indian was being deprived of education to let Chander be in school. Chand's interpretation was different. To him it was a case of limited educational facilities at that point in time causing many take such an unreasonable position. This was totally rejected by his classmates for as they said to him, later on in life, commensurate to education, suitable employment had to be provided to him in the deprivation of another who was more eligible from residency point of view. Obviously, this was another criterion. To have the economy grow to a level that there was no such unemployment problem was obviously a distant goal, so far away that nobody talked about it not even the planning commission of the country. Of course going abroad was welcomed as everyone used to say then, it meant valuable foreign exchange to the country. Foreign remittances were making sizeable contribution to the coiffures of the country. Chandu, as he was called, found his way by staying quiet, hardly ever talking to anyone. He concentrated on his books. So much so that he started reading other textbooks on his chosen subjects to excel.

Now he had overcome many delusions. Things he did not understand hitherto were now fitting in, to a rational and coherent manner. Ask not as a right but seek consideration on merit. The colour of his glasses had been shed. But it seemed to have been replaced by a new colour. Was the new colour the right and real colour. If he moved to a new environment of place and people, would he still perceive things in the same manner. To Chand it was a situation that had arisen caused by his beliefs which were largely self-serving due the given conditions with respect to his age, his need to continue his schooling and the all-important need to get along with his classmates. After some more time when he would have finished his eleventh, he will have graduated, the outward existing influences will have weakened, and new forces shall emerge. Would he still see the same picture or will a new picture emerge in its place. Will the new picture bring about similar responses of anxiety, fear, anger, and jealousy. Will he have to work on his states of mind once again and one by one dismiss them as figments of blurred vision. By reasoning he avoided any anxiety. For Chander, there was nothing to fear when he had no ill will. He stayed away from negative people. Chander was always in competition with himself. To him there was no cause to be jealous. With new horizons, new vistas, and new hope there was no cause to be angry. Just a lot to learn and with a positive attitude he moved forward confidently.

Chapter III

College

Years 1964 to 1969

After Chand's excellent performance in the Higher Secondary School examination, people started calling him Chander. His parents preferred to have him go to a distant premier institute to study Mechanical Engineering. Here, he found the atmosphere completely different. Till now, he had known people mostly of his own kind. The capital city of Delhi had provided him an opportunity to know some people from other parts of India. Interaction with them was limited. Apart from the fact that their food habits and the manner they ate their food was different, like those around him, he never showed any interest to know any one closely. Now things were different. Chander himself was, one of many, from other parts of the country. Indeed, their different habits, unique way of thinking and the manner they perceived things was not what he was accustomed to. He had read and heard different things regarding their language, culture, and the history of the regions they came from. Now it was all there and each one of them was proud of their own background. The patriotic zeal as proud Indians united them to be one people, determined to build India. They prayed to be good citizens worthy of being honoured.

Chander would feel amused that he was a raw material. He was to graduate as a finished product. When he would go to work in industry, he would once again be a raw material, being paid for the promise he held that with his sound background, and in reasonable time, he will be an asset to the company he worked for. Indeed many of its alumnus had become columns on which their organisations stood. So there was a legacy to be preserved. He was now a part of that promise to his country. The very thought of it, gave him a sense of satisfaction and a reason to strive.

Chander found getting to know other students and talking about things in a new manner was totally mind boggling. Their way of looking at events of past and present and on many issues seemed to be radically different. Chander wondered if his thinking was narrow minded. Was he slow to grasp the different interpretations. Each one of them looked at everything from his own background where he came from. When he found his own way of looking at practices, happenings and the way things went on was entirely different. He began to wonder, was he highly opinionated and self-centred, too rigid to accept the diversity. To live with it was indeed different from merely reading or discussing about it. But soon, particularly with those in his own hall of residence, a new camaraderie was to emerge. As friends they discussed everything- their subjects, their experiences, their customs, traditions and what not. Many had a strong feeling, that we all were part of a chain, and the strength of the chain was its weakest link. So we were all one and yet so different staying steadfast in our pursuit.

Chander had given up taking time to do his meditation, his yoga and allowing himself time to ensure his own bearings. He. worked in the hostel gymnasium (Akhara) in the evening. A few minutes on the horizontal bar and the parallel bar were sufficient to keep him fit. Chander never went for weightlifting.

He began to like some friends. Many he detested. Indeed he was very jealous of many. Chander understood that in many areas of interest, he lagged behind so much that he was developing a hostile attitude. His own limitation to pick up fast was due to his own late start and a lack of exposure to many extra curricular activities. Arranging meals for nearly three hundred students required estimate of ingredients, stored and fresh, everyday. Then the cooking of East Indian, North Indian, and South Indian food everyday to a plat-able level was indeed a challenge. The secretary's charge for a quarter exposed him to his own inadequate knowledge. A running mess with a full time Manager and an Assistant Manager would continue to function normally with or without the Secretary. The challenge was, what you could bring to its normal functioning, whether with respect to ingredients, way of cooking or serving or to raise the hygienic standard and so fore. Chander found that there was a lot to learn. Deteriorated eggs, stale vegetables, partially black onions, past expiry date tinned food etc. pertained to the supply side. Use of refined and double refined oil indiscriminately called for monitoring. Chander was told that issue had already been resolved by his predecessors - the purees tasted better in double refined oil. There was little contribution that Chander could make. In the hygienic area Chander tried the one station approach. For example live chickens were received. Their heads were chopped off, anywhere in the kitchen where the cooks could catch them running. They would then be taken to the designated area for cleaning and cutting to pieces. The entire kitchen would be a bloody mess. Several – up to four men had to spend an hour cleaning the mess. As regards to the feelings of the vegetarians, the less said the better. Chander suggested that we buy some chicken baskets and receive the chickens in them. The suppliers would not part with their special chicken baskets. Then from the baskets at the assigned area, chickens could be taken one by one and cut, cleaned and pieces be made. Chander's desire to learn about the spices and how they were applied in cooking remained unrealised. For one thing Chander could have only so much time set aside for mess matters and furthermore the next quarter, a new Secretary was to take over. Chander humorously remarked that he would share the zeal of Columbus and Vasco da Gama some other time. A friend of his remarked that Constantinople will not fall again. Well traitors have appeared throughout the history. May be someone will leave the door open again. Lastly the one thing that he felt called for examining was that the staff of the mess, cooks, and bearers, worked from seven in the morning to nine thirty at night with a three hours break in the afternoon. This made a eleven and half hours of work per day with no Sunday. Nobody wants to rock the boat. Labour was available in abundance. One could not go by merely demand and supply. Yet no realistic, nor acceptable solution could be found. Any solution discussed to mitigate the hardship would result in a quantum jump in the monthly mess bill. The government was setting up ITI's including for catering discipline, all over the country. But its students and graduates had high sights. If they were not looking forward to going abroad or working in top notch hotels, they were preferring to be entrepreneurs. Chander did not feel anything could be done for quite some time. Was he right. Was he wrong. Perhaps his view was wrong. If it was not practical to have an eight-hour shift, a staggered hourly schedule, could have been experimented with. A twenty to thirty percent increase in workforce, working on staggered hours would have been more humane. His wrong view of nothing could be done was indeed shameful and reckless.

Some of his seniors wanted him to represent the block in Intra Hall quiz. Chander felt too restless. His encyclopaedic knowledge was poor. It was with much difficulty that he was able to get himself excused. Later on he realised his mistake. He would have been backed by his block mates and indeed it would have been a wonderful experience.

Another interesting experience that Chander had that he was never to forget. It was the annual declamation contest. Some of his close friends managed to get his name on the list of the Hall. A select number of students from each Hall of Residence on campus were to represent their Hall. Chander felt elated. He thought about the topic and made some notes. Next day, a hallmate came to his room. He handed him a few long sheets and said to him, "Here is your speech". Surprised Chander remarked that he had made his notes and now had to expand them. Chander assured him that he would include all the points that were there in the sheets that he had given. His friend found his remark very unpleasant. With a stern face he left without uttering a word. Next day Chander met him outside the dining room. He said to Chander it was alright. "You can write in your own words." Chander felt a huge relief. Before he could write the full speech with two inputs, his own and his friends, a Telugu wing mate came to him and gave him some notes to consider while preparing the draft. Soon everybody in the Hall got to know about it. Chander was summarily told to forget about the speech. Chander was shocked. It was on behalf of the entire hall that he was going to speak. What was wrong in his having a third input. Chander was not being like the king of France, Louis XIV, who had to strongly assert that he was not king of Paris, he was king of France and so he built Versailles, which was to remain capital of France for over a hundred years. A day later, he found himself reading the Notice Board. Chander had stopped reading the Notice Board regularly. Anyway, the annual contest had been opened to all students. Now he could participate. Several hundred registered themselves. The absenteeism was heavy.

Chander's participation was for some reason without the enthusiasm. He did not have his heart into it. Chander was the seventy fifth speaker. Many of the points he wanted to elaborate on had been dealt extensively by previous speakers. He merely reinforced those reasons and made his speech short and pithy. His call for living many of the assertions he made was appreciated.

Chander had been driven into an introspective examination of himself. Was it better to be honest with yourself and live by what you believe to be honest, just, and fair. Or should you consider being part of the group as of paramount importance and toe the group line sincerely. Chander found it terribly difficult to decide. In general the group or the organisation matters. But it is the individual that makes the difference. Then sticking to yours beliefs called for a price to be paid. Sacrifice was an important feature in such an assertion, particularly if you are in a minority. It continued to occupy Chander's mind, so much so that he found it hard to concentrate on his course. Weeks later it suddenly dawned on him that whether it was he or someone else, you had to work your way to that position at which you can make the changes. There did not seem to be any other way. And so for Chander another building block had come up.

He picked up his copy of Gitanjali by Rabindranath Tagore to get his agitated mind a change. One quote,

"Pluck this little flower and take it, delay not! I fear lest it droop and drop into dust.

It may not find a place in thy garland, but honour it with a touch of pain from thy hand and pluck it. I fear lest the day end before I am aware, and the time of offering go by.

Though its colour be not deep and it's smell be faint, use this flower in thy service and pluck it while there is time."

Imagining the flower to an idea that has blossomed in your mind, Chander felt that when an idea comes one must grab it. There is nothing stronger than an idea whose time has come. If we can seize it, be a part of it and become that idea itself, we stand a good chance to do ourselves justice and contribute to the society. Everyone has many chances, only we have to be tuned to that wavelength to grasp it. Further what we do, whether we sew it in a garland or make an offering at the prayer or work it around to our advantage it is up to us. Many would pin it on their jacket to some association.

Chapter IV

After College

Years 1969 to 1970

Chander or Mr. Finished Product was now ready once again to be a raw material. He had learnt during his Practical Training that all successful companies flourished by culture. Not only their designs, production techniques but also, under the law, their work force had to be closely watched. A large measure of the success of the organisations depended on its employees motivation. Once he joined an organisation and became an employee he would be immersed in the new challenges. So he began to enjoy with his Delhi friends who had graduated with him. One of his school and college friend from Delhi counselled him that it was only for a few months he could go on like that. In case he decided to pursue post-graduation program, he gave Chander a list of the names and addresses of Universities in USA that had accepted from our Institute, students for admission to post graduate courses. Chander could now request prospectus and admission forms. Those days GRE was required to study for master's and or Doctoral programs in American Universities.

Chander's friend was darned right. Three or four months later, with no future plans and no employment, he started feeling low. Chander found himself getting irritated often. His own mind was not clear. On one hand, he was applying for admission abroad for post-graduation. On the other he was applying for MBA course. What more, he enrolled himself for a crash course in German at the Max Mueller House. Chander was open for a good employment too. Indeed he did not have any focus. His vision was getting blurred. Not knowing what he exactly wanted was indeed unfortunate. Till now, most of such decisions were made by his parents. He now had to make his own choice, whether to go in for manufacturing, design or building and operating power plants or space research etc. His own reservoir of 'Inner Resources' was getting depleted. Chander was finding difficulty in maintaining the positive mind, he was accustomed to. He had to make a choice from what was available to him. Once the die was cast, there was very little choice. This he understood very well.

Before graduating, he had a few job offers but they were all in the Eastern side of the country. Chander thought something would work out in the Northern Zone. Chander recalled what a South Indian schoolfriend, Kappu had said to him five years earlier. On learning that Chander had opted to go to big institute in Eastern India, Kappu considered going to a local college where Chander had already got admission based on his performance in Higher Secondary Examination a better choice. To Chander, Kappu was saying, "Kaun Jai Delhi ki Galian Chor kar". So Chander disregarded Kappu then. Now Chander realised the ramifications, in full dimension, of Kappu's assertion.

Chapter V

Taking Up A Job

Year 1970

Chander had applied for admission to some universities in USA for Post Graduate program, but it was too early for a reply. He had now begun to look actively for employment. Fortunately Chander got a break. He was offered employment by a large company, closer to his university he had graduated from than his hometown. It did not seem to matter then. He decided to join. Not realising that it was a carrier job and that he was expected to remain there, if not for his entire work life, at least for five to six years. This had created some problems for him. He surveyed around to see what life would be like, but could not find himself to like it or not like it. He had an eye opener when he took a French station leave on one Sunday during his training program and went to sit in a competition examination of Calcutta institute of management. The following Monday, Chander was called by the training manager and told if he wanted to take some course, he should talk to him and not go anywhere. To Chander, this was the first introduction to the concept of being under an in charge. Terribly stifling. So Chander had felt. A cousin's husband who worked for a sister company or reverse, his company was a sister company of the one his brother-in-law worked for, lived close by. Chander started spending most of his free time with them. He enjoyed the company of the engineers of the Company, he worked for. All the trainee engineers were housed in the Engineers Hall. With a common mess, plenty of opportunity was there to know them but the mini groups that had sprung up were mostly on linguistic lines. For some reason, he did not have his heart in to it. This was even though he found some of his new acquaintances to be very fine people, always friendly, cooperative, and ready to help. One time he felt he was taking them for granted because he was always taking off to his sisters residence.

A little over five months of his with the Company, Chander got the letter of his acceptance in the Post Graduate program of the California State University at Los Angeles in California. He talked to his close friends who worked with him. His friends suggested to him not to talk or discuss with anyone and quietly leave. It was indeed an opportunity for him. They all agreed on this. It was of no use giving any one a chance to talk him out of it. So he packed his bags and left for Delhi. It was made possible with the help and cooperation of some of his friends and colleagues. In Delhi Chander got busy with getting a passport, visa and ticket which took a couple of weeks. Everything was well timed and planned so that Chander would reach Los Angeles a few days before the Fall Quarter began in the University he was going to.

Chapter VI

Journey To Abroad

Year 1971

The Air Lines for a long journey passenger allowed a couple of lay overs, as they called them. On his way to Los Angeles from New Delhi, Chander stayed nearly a day in Hong Kong. Well planned and developed four islands constituting Hong Kong were to be handed over to the Chinese in another generation. To Chander the apprehensions of the local people was unfounded. Surely something could be worked out to allow them to retain their identity. The local group of people did not think much of Chander giving them hope. They said, "Look at Tibet. Why would Hong Kong be different". "Our businesses, our properties and so fore will be all gone. The Communists will take everything. Our culture, our way of life will be gone for ever. What will happen to our children? No religion." Chander did not understand why they were talking to him on this subject since he was not in politics and was a student of engineering going for further studies to USA. Chander excused himself as a tourist. Well they said, "Think about it, friend". Chander now felt that they were appealing for help. Knowing the Britishers, to them it is an agreement they opined. They further said as Easterners they valued life differently. After being mauled in 1962, there was very little India could do to help. Family after family of Hong Kong Chinese was preparing to migrate to West. A great shopping centre's fate was in jeopardy. To the West it was an agreement that had to be honoured. Agreements with Communists were a matter of convenience as far as they, the communists, were concerned. No agreement was binding on them. Anyway, this had taken Chander's mind off from what it was occupied with- his folks back in India and his curriculum for the post-graduation.

Chander's next stop was Tokyo. What a contrast. No comparison with India also. The clean and serene environment even in the hustle and bustle of marketplace was extraordinary. No irate nor any violent people were to be seen. Chander, as a foreigner, a tourist, found them very polite, courteous, and helpful. What was astounding was how the Japanese treated their own kind. Their mild demeanour was their hallmark. Chander decided to do some shopping. At a large departmental store, a Japanese suggested to Chander that he study in Tokyo and not go to USA. A surprised Chander took a few seconds to grasp it. The Osaka fair was going on and many tourists from India were there. Anyway, Chander declined the offer. Chander proceeded to pay for his wristwatch he had bought but they suggested him to just take it. Chander could not understand, why a freebie. A store employee explained that for a tourist, the purchase was excise free. To ring the sale, an enormous paperwork was required, and for such a small sale, it was not justifiable. Chander smiled. Then a Japanese customer, who spoke English very well remarked, "The Prime Ministerial candidate Shinzo Abe is in the store. So the store is crowded." Chander felt that was education for him. Abe was the anointed one. Or perhaps the Japanese were telling him, it is already written. Indians are not the only ones who have the destiny planned. Anyway Abe bowed to Chander and Chander bowed in return. The atmosphere became different. Later Abe, as Prime Minister of Japan visited India and with Prime Minister Modi made time to attend the special ceremony at the religious city of Varanasi.

The next leg of his journey took him to Honolulu. Many people long for a vacation in Hawaii. Chander felt elated that he was in Honolulu. He left his baggage in a locker at the airport and went straight to the beach. It was fantastic. The clear blue water and long wide beach was inviting. What more all along the beach, a lane for pedestrians to stroll was maintained so clean that for someone from India it was surprising. Very few people were there at the beach. Chander saw only one more man walking the pedestrian way at a distance from him. In his mind, Chander compared the beach with the beaches in Madras, now Chennai and Bombay, now Mumbai. Apparently we had done a good job rechristening them but maintaining them was a different matter. He compared it with the Digha Beach in West Bengal. The sea there in India is comparatively very rough and not low but high waves, several feet high, could be seen reaching the beach even in daytime. Chander learnt that the beaches in Hawaii were naturally blue and the sea quiet. Chander found it incredible. At that time, he could not fathom how the sea was so quiet. Later when he found the beaches in California also quiet, he learnt that wave breakers way out in the sea was the reason.

Chander crossed the international date line over the Pacific Ocean and was now on the last leg of his journey. From Hawaii to Los Angeles was a local flight as he had already entered the

United States at Honolulu. Most of the passengers were going to San Francisco. A fellow passenger Chander got acquainted with remarked, "People go to Los Angeles to go to Hollywood and not for studies". From New Orleans, since the 20's, it was Hollywood that was the centre of the tinsel world and the actors lived in Hollywood hills. Chander had not given this a thought while deciding to go to Los Angeles.

Chapter VII

American University Campus

Year 1971

On reaching Los Angeles airport, instead of proceeding straight to the University campus Chander decided to stop at the residence of a family friend hailing from the same colony where Chander grew up in Delhi. The Comar's had emigrated a few years earlier. They made Chander feel at home. Chander felt like he was still in India. Earlier on landing at the airport, he had felt a little nervous. Chander was now in a new city in a new country and a going to a foreign university. Chander looked at it as a new opportunity and a chance to make a new beginning. Indeed, it was so. At Comar uncles house, a good bath and a filling Indian lunch made Chander feel comfortable. Chander was now ready to proceed to the campus of his new university. Comar Uncle Ji was very nice. He asked him to relax for he and Aunty Ji were going to drop him at the campus in their car. This indeed was very nice of them and very Indian like. Chander had earlier been advised not to accept such favours as the busy life in USA did not allow anyone to spare time for something like that without causing inconvenience to those around them. Nearly an hour and half drive got Chander to the campus. He thanked them and they left.

At first Chander was overjoyed. There were three apartment buildings at a walking distance from the university campus. It was America, so the buildings were University approved, but private. The university itself was a Government University. As Chander walked towards the buildings, an Indian student from Gujarat saw him. Since Chander was walking with his bags (later Chander found that it was very unusual) he asked Chander, "Have you just arrived from India". Chander told him that he had and was looking for an apartment. He was very friendly and helpful. He took Chander to his apartment and offered some tonic water. In a few minutes they became friends. He made some phone calls to the building managers to find out about vacancy, as it was termed. In his own building, there was none. He called an Indian friend, only to learn there was no vacancy in his building also. So only the third building was left. Fortunately, this building had a vacancy, but the Manager wanted a reference from someone living in the building. This was arranged and Chander checked in. It was all Indians helping one another, in this case a newcomer from India. Chander began to remember his own hostel and friends in the Indian University he studied. He felt very comfortable now. He had made some friends. They helped Chander find his way in the apartment building, college, and stores nearby. Everybody had to make own arrangement for cooking. Facilities like gas, oven and fridge etc. were available in a furnished apartment. A bed with a mattress and a study table were all there.

The next day Chander's friend took him to the bank to take care of matters as required in USA. Chander cashed all the traveller cheque's and on the way back, bought the pots and pans along with groceries. Day after that he went to the University Campus and completed the Registration requirements and paid the tuition fees. The classes were to begin in two days, but Chander felt acclimatised and all-ready to go. He discussed the courses like Machine Design or Heat Transfer with his new friends, who were his seniors, and made up his mind before he met his advisor. His choice was Heat Transfer major and Fluid Flow minor.

The high standard of cleanliness coupled with self-discipline to maintain that, was a way of life. Chander too had to keep a few things in his mind all the time. New habits as he called them were the new way. Everything seemed to be different or opposite. Pushing the switch up meant on. Traffic moved on the right. This quite often caused confusion as to which side of the road to wait for the bus. Private cars and taxi seemed to be the common mode of transport. The bus service was terrible. It was essentially for elderly and handicapped. Some regular commuters had adjusted themselves. Generally, the city was well spread, and public transport plied on major arteries only. Slowly, Chander began to get acclimatised to new way as that was the way.

Chapter VIII

First Quarter

Year 1971

The first quarter, which is the fall quarter at the university was over. Concentrating on his studies only, brought Chander three A's and one B. For such a satisfactory performance, the University kept the miscellaneous charges and refunded the fee to foreign students. Great. A few foreign students from India were working in the library. Chander talked to them and when in need, he got himself a job to work ten to fifteen hours a week. More than the money, to Chander a job in the campus gave him an opportunity to meet different people and interact with them. Chander learnt the Library of Congress system which was now becoming the new standard system. The out of vogue, Dewey Decimal system was still in use. Also Chander felt at home in the library to find some material by subject or author or going through the Indexes. Later during the course, when he had to do Graduate Research Study Chander found it easy to find the publications on the subject in the technical journals. Since Chander had not taken interest in the library at the Graduate level, although the facilities were there, he had compensated himself.

Chander continued to wear his Indian clothes, stitched Indian style. This was not common. Most of the foreign students had switched to American style clothes. Many had started going Bowling, or play Pool or started going for camping. Chander was from a river culture. Delhi is at the right bank of Yamuna. All the same Chander had begun to enjoy going to the beach with friends. In India, he had never gone horse racing and betting, though some of his friends used to go frequently to bet. Nor did he know anything about the horses. Anyway, he went once in Los Angeles. Before the races began, Chander saw many people go near the horses to inspect them. They were all examining the teeth of the horses. At first Chander, did not understand. Then he remembered the old saying, "Never look at a gift horse in the mouth." Obviously, they were estimating the age of the horses they were going to bet on. Perhaps that was not all there was to it. An old man seeing us novices, quipped, "Lose a tooth and have your horse win". Chander did not know how. All the same he would rather lose the bet than lose a tooth.

The international atmosphere that Chander was in, provided him with an opportunity to meet students from many other countries. There were, Koreans, Filipinos, Palestinians, Arabs, and Jews. They all belonged to category called Asian and Pacific Islanders. Chander was not used to seeing himself as an Asian. He was an Indian of Indian origin. Chander looked at Indian matters from the angle of emergence of Europe in the life of Asia. This he coupled with the frequent complaints of the intelligentsia of India that all our matters, including establishing of our national borders is done by the Europeans. The Indians were never given a chance. However, the fact remained that most of our own bilateral or multilateral agreements with our neighbours tended to have a short life. The Arabs were very friendly with Indians. Chander wondered, how much of it had to do with the refusal of India to recognise the State of Israel. Most of the Arabs that Chander met had an obsession to destroy Israel. The Arabs were very emotional and would get worked up very fast on this issue. The reason was obvious. The displaced Palestinians had been trampled over. They were uprooted. For the Arabs, the Palestinians were their own kind and felt a strong feeling of Brotherhood with them. They were of one stock with strong social, cultural, and religious ties. Chander remembered what Mahatma Gandhi had said. "If the cause is just, why are guns being used". Everyone knows that the State of Israel was created with British guns after the end of World War II. Somehow and for what reason, Chander wondered why nobody talked of that. Perhaps it was too early for that. The Jewish students he found were occupied with the experimental university offering course in Hebrew. The Experimental University was a new feature that Chander found interesting. In India, the courses offered to the students were by and large, the choice of the faculty. Most of the courses were in line with Western Universities. In the USA, every university had an Experimental College. A group of students or a foundation could offer a free course (with the permission of Administration of University). If the response was good the course would get included in the curriculum. So this was how the new courses were introduced. Interestingly, Chander met a middle-aged man from India in the campus. He was Vice Chancellor of Osmania University in Hyderabad who had come under the exchange program to learn about the Administration of Universities in USA. Chander met him for a few minutes. Somehow, he left an impression that Chander did not forget. Also, there was a

Fulbright scholar from Punjab University in Chandigarh. His field was Sociology. A little elder to us, he mixed with other students from India during his short stay. The Chinese students were different. Chander found them to be of two kinds, the American and Foreign Students like him. One Chinese student said to him, "We are different. We are American Chinese; you are Indian American." To Chander it meant that this Chinese could trace his American ancestors for generations. Also it meant that they were first American and then Chinese. For Indians in America, they could not go as American Indian, for American Indian meant Red Indians, the original people who inhabited America. Was he joking or was he making a point. Soon he became a friend. Indians in America are mostly known as East Indians. Interestingly, Chander learnt about the Melting Pot of America. Those who migrated to America before the last war were now Americans. They ceased to have any other identity. They were simply Americans. Later when Chander met an elderly man who was originally from India and had emigrated in early thirties insisted that he was an American and did not belong to the Asian and Pacific Islander category, the melting pot theory was corroborated. But ever since the last war, the melting pot has been out of fuel.

Many of Chander's friends lived in the apartment building for a quarter term of the university. At the end of the quarter, the locals would go home. Next quarter they rented a new accommodation. Chander had lengthy discussions with a foreign Chinese student (they were mostly from KMT China). The Chinese surprised Chander by recalling the dark ages opined that the Americans or for that matter the so-called Westerns would not give the Chinese a chance. We, the Indians could try. In the light of what many Americans believe that the

Indian civilisation is an offshoot of the Chinese civilisation and the fact that in America Indian table is under the Chinese table, Chander wondered, was it a matter for him to laugh off or it deserved a serious thought. Chander left it at that for the time being. The Koreans and other students from South East Asia, to Chander were very reserved and seemed to enjoy with their own kind. Other students from India did not share his view. It seemed; each had his own experience. One student from Philippines, with whom Chander shared his apartment, was very outward. Always looking for fun, he was a very joyous guy. But Chander had to do some justice to his studies also. So Chander did not join him often. The Pakistanis and Indians had a separate equation. Many felt that all attempts to find a separate identity for Pakistanis and Indians in the subcontinent were futile. For there was none. There were yet others, who felt that Indians could not accept emotionally, and many mentally too, the creation and the existence of a separate State of Pakistan. Pakistan, unlike India had a special relationship with USA. It was by virtue of the military alliance; Pakistan enjoyed a separate and special relationship. All the same, by and large, if a Pakistani student could help a student from India, he was not found wanting. But they would not talk about it. Chander once had an inkling that Pakistanis ran the risk of inviting the displeasure of their own kind if they socialised with those from India.

Chapter IX

Venturing Outside the Campus

Year 1971

Chander wanted to know more about the Americans. Not confining himself to the campus life, Chander ventured to take up a twenty hours a week, part time regular job, in downtown Los Angeles. The job had been advertised on the university's notice board. This was an odd job for Chander. It was not related to engineering. He worked as a Salesclerk. Going to downtown changed his routine and Chander enjoyed it. Chander began to know people he worked with and found it an experience. At Chander's level most were younger but those who had worked for the Departmental Store for years gave him some insight to their lives. Their culture was different, and their approach was new to him. The most common book everyone talked about was, 'How to win friends and influence people' by Dale Carnegie. Some of the short stories of O. Henry's (William Sydney Porter) were being lived around. It took some careful observation and thought to see that quite a few young men were from Pakistan. They helped Chander have a deep understanding of the

American culture. In an outward smiling and happy facade were many struggles and resolves Chander had not imagined. Mark Twain's characters were also quoted in general talk. The war in Vietnam was still going on. Chander remembered 1962 and 1965 wars in India. Then also he was a student. How his patriotic spirit had made him feel, Chander had a vivid recollection. While in India, Madam Indira Gandhi, our Prime Minister, had her sympathies with the so-called Vietcong, and called their leader 'Uncle Ho', in USA the mothers were getting their sons back in 'Plastic Bags'. Those who were dying for their country - America, had families, wives, and children. Now, there were war widows and orphans. The enormous initiative and effort of the private organisations, social and commercial (Big, Small American, and multinational corporations) was to Chander exemplary and to be emulated. To the Americans, the President was supreme and a call from the President made all Americans to fall in line. That's how their system had evolved. At first Chander found it unusual. But then he remembered the way Indians rallied behind Nehru and how the political leaders had sunk their differences in 1962 or the manner in which the Egyptians backed Gamal Abdul Nasser after the fall of Sinai Peninsula in the Six-Day War with Israel in 1967, and caused his reinstatement by popular demonstrations. While the establishment of America was behind the President, the young students and hippies were organising calls to end the Vietnam war. Chander wondered what was in the best interest of India. Chander felt that in the broader context, America was fighting India's war to contain China. The manner in which the Chinese expansionism had taken place and what more its consolidation, in Xinjiang Uygur, Tibet(Xizang), Inner Mongolia, Guangxi and Ningxia. These groups were for all practical purposes forgotten. Chander was well aware of the Chinese demand of five fingers Ladakh, Nepal, Sikkim, Bhutan, and Arunachal Pradesh. It's territorial ambitions included Myanmar, Cambodia, Laos, and Vietnam. Chander wondered, if race was the sole consideration for the making of a nation as the Chinese claim was founded on, then all of the Africa should be one nation. Also, Europe should be one nation. Had USA not participated in the last war and confined itself to containing Japan only, Hitler's dream of a Unified Europe under Germany would have been realised. Indeed Hitler would have become Otto Von Bismarck or Sardar Patel of Europe. The Americans have an enormous respect for the Chinese Culture and their business acumen. As a Chinese story goes a king of China once said, "If a cat jumps to the throne of the king of China, the cat does not become the king". "Then who is the king", he was asked. "The king is the one who is worrying about food for his people" the king replied. Indeed that is very profound. But that does not mean that ten percent of the agricultural population should be in possession of two thirds of the land of entire China. Surely that paves the way for a rebellion or even a revolution. Chander felt that it was something for him to remember with respect of his own country of India. He recalled, how the Nehru Government in 1951 abolished the zamindari system, whence the tiller became owner of the land he cultivated.

Another thing Chander saw was the occupation of so many Americans with self-improvement programs. The new techniques and ways of self-improvement were very popular with Americans of all ages. They were open to Yoga, Meditation, Chinese acupuncture and acupressure, dangerous hypnotism and so on. The college graduates talked of transactional analysis, self-actualisation, living a life of gratitude etcetera. To Chander it was all looking inward and not outward for their own peace of mind, satisfaction, and happiness. There were so many casualties

- resorting to booze and drugs that the Government was funding rehabilitation programs all over the country. In a fast-changing technology, new innovations, and new ways of doing things, there was a good percentage of Americans who had to retrain themselves for new jobs and new competition in their work life. This brought about many new pressures and new adjustments in a fast-changing society. Chander began to wonder if such a fast pace of life was introduced in India what would happen. Were India to progress rapidly and adopt new technologically advanced techniques the inevitable problems in the social and cultural field were difficult to imagine. The low literacy level of the masses was not providing a conducive environment. Primitive social practices would subject the society, particularly the women, to a greater exploitation resulting in an unmanageable social problems and even an upheaval. There was one thing Chander had learnt well and that summed up the American scene. The best answer to any problem came from people engaged in the profession to which the problem belonged. One way of saying this is, they are qualified in their field, so they have earned the right to recommend the solution or answer to the problem. What more, it was their domain to recommend the rapidity of its (solution) implementation. To Chander this was the key to a speedier technological, economic, and social progress of the country.

Chapter X

Memorable Dinner

Year 1972

This was all very fine. Downtown had provided him an opportunity to grow rapidly. But it had taken its toll on his grades- his performance in studies had fallen. So, Chander quit his odd job to go back to college with full course load in the next quarter. Chander made up his mind to concentrate on his studies for the next two quarters. Chander moved to the adjoining apartment building where, while he shared his apartment with another student, assigned by the Manager of the building, Chander had a separate bedroom. All this Chander did to make change in style and pace.

Chander spent most of his time at the university. He could not concentrate on his books in his apartment. This apartment building had a much more social life. Distractions were many. He was in the library for hours and would eat at the university cafeteria. One day, the Indian origin friend Ash from Chandigarh who was also his senior at the University, invited him for a dinner. Ash was having an American friend with his family come over and I was also invited. Ash had been Chander's friend, from day one Chander had landed in Los Angeles. Ash had been very helpful. From finding a vacancy, to finding a reference in the building Chander lived earlier, or going for a haircut or going to the bank in the shopping complex at a distance, Ash was always willing. The market and stores were far flung. At that time Chander did not have car of his own and went along at the convenience of those who had. Public transport had a low frequency, once every hour and therefore inconvenient. Sometimes Chander wondered, how was Ash of such a helpful nature. Was he gifted by nature or had he worked hard to acquire it. Chander was not the only one Ash helped. Ash used to help so many Indian students that he was not only popular but also had many friends. Ash was envied.

Anyway, Chander got ready for the evening. Normally, Chander would have been suited, booted but for some reason he preferred to go in a casual evening wear. That was the custom in Los Angeles. When Chander got there, the main guest was already there. The discussion was interrupted for a few seconds to introduce him. The American, as Chander learnt had a business. He had a large work force of nearly fifty people working for him. The American guest continued. "Knowledge of books or degrees was not the only thing that mattered. Knowledge of the subject is essential for doing a good job. But it is the attitude that is of essence. I can take a man in (meaning employment) with the right attitude but no knowledge of the subject. I can train him. Whereas a man who knows the job but does not have the right attitude, he is of no use to me. I cannot change the attitude of a person." His wife quipped, "Dan you can try." In a cool manner he replied, "Anything is possible except that it takes a lot of time and effort. It costs money to do that. Usually it is not worth." Dinner would take a few minutes. My friend himself was the Chef. The discussion suddenly turned to Kashmir. The American remarked that Kashmir was part of Pakistan. Taking into view that the overwhelmingly large population of Kashmir was Muslims, and its contiguity justified its inclusion in Pakistan. He continued that as Pakistan was an ally of USA, the military alliance caused his choice. This was too much for Chander. His face showed it and he felt difficult to breath. He came out of the apartment to get some fresh air. Somebody hollered, "Dinner is ready" and Chander went back in. Everybody enjoyed the dinner. Chicken, fish, and cauliflower were delicious. Dinner was followed by American Ice Cream and liqueur. Chander neither joined for drinks before dinner nor did he have liqueur. He enjoyed the ice cream. American ice cream was different. It was richer in cream -very, very rich. There was no taste of milk. One has to eat to know the difference. Then the Americans left. They had a well over an hour's drive to get home. Later, Chander walked home telling himself that a man should know his limitations. Him losing his composure, when he heard Kashmir was not a part of India, was his immaturity. No reason is good enough to get worked up even if you hear something you find outlandish. Not everyone looks at things as you do. It would be naive to think in that manner. As the Chinese Premier, Chou en Lai said, "There is no feeling too big for words. Every feeling can be translated into words." So Chander tried to give an expression to his strong feelings that evening. Having grown up in India and for the first time ventured outside the country, his thinking was conditioned in a particular manner. However on this sensitive matter and many more, there could not be any compromise. Yet, however, an outward show of emotions and sentiments was not called for. In a firm manner and without mincing words, one should convey ones positions and if possible give reasons for it. He further formulated his thoughts on this Kashmir issue. The signing of the instrument of accession of Kashmir by the Maharaja Hari Singh was necessary before the Indian troops could march in. The Maharaja did that and that made all other considerations irrelevant. Rest was history. Mahatma Gandhi's intervention and Sardar Patels helplessness in that wake had led to a partition of the Jammu and Kashmir state like Punjab and West Bengal. It was difficult to change that now. Also, India was a secular country and had over thirty-five million Muslims then in 1947 and now two hundred and four million; the reasoning of the American did not carry any weight. So a partition along the LOC with minor adjustments (which is the position of India) is perfectly in order. Chander said to himself that he would have to do his homework and plan some thinking and study if necessary, on many matters, personal and public. He did not have to be dumbfounded on hearing something that was totally displeasing to him. In short, he had to re-examine his life, his views, opinion and perhaps way of doing things. Chander knew that on many matters, his thinking had changed considerably. He looked at many social, cultural, religious practices in the background of the countries people came from. The mainstream American culture was vastly different and hence different viewpoints were inevitable. He sought refuge in what Mahatma Gandhi said about his evolving and changing views on many matters. He had said, "If you trust my sanity, you go by my latter view". So it was part of the ever growing and learning process in everyone's life.

Chapter XI

Brother Visits

Year 1972

One long weekend suddenly Chander's elder brother Mohan who was living in Midwest Chicago, came to visit him. He stayed with him for three days. On the first day Mohan went sightseeing Los Angeles in the tourist buses by himself. On the second day, Mohan and Chander together took a fight to Las Vegas, a city known all over the world for its gambling casinos, fine dining and entertainment, luxurious hotels, and night life. They spent the morning and early afternoon visiting casinos. While visitors played many types of games, Chander played the slot machines and roulette only. American card games like poker and blackjack were new to him. Anyway to Chander, it was to enjoy and lose money. He saw a look of anxiety on some faces, who were betting heavy. There seemed to be people from all over the world gathered to gamble their money away. There were many casinos, mostly in a cluster. A couple of them were at a walking distance away. While most of the people were busy gambling, there were singers and comedians performing in the casinos. While some were established artists, there were many newcomers performing to display their skill and trying their luck. To Chander it seemed many a new artist had made a humble beginning in the casinos. Indeed Las Vegas was the Entertainment Capital of the world. Chander noticed many advertisement signs inviting people for a quick divorce. The six weeks residency requirement of Nevada, the state in which Las Vegas was located, gave liberal laws for legal separation. To Chander, coming from India, it was of academic interest.

In the afternoon they took a twenty-five-seater turbo prop plane to Grand Canyon. It is a steep sided canyon, nearly three hundred miles long, eighteen miles wide and has a depth of nearly a mile. Colorado river runs at its bottom. In India, in the foothills of Himalayan mountains, are many river valleys. The sheer size of the Grand Canyon made it great. Chander and his brother looked at the Colorado flowing from the top only. One could walk down but coming up would be an enormous task or they would have to hire a mule. To the American Indians, living at the bottom of the canyon on the banks of Colorado, running nearly in the middle of the valley, was a routine. They walked up and down the passage that had been created by their footprints. It was an equivalent of a 'Pagdandi' in India. The American Indian tribe of Hopi inhabited it. The Puebloans were the natives prior to its discovery. Late afternoon, they took a flight back to Los Angeles.

Chander's brother surprised him prior to his departure back to Chicago. Mohan made it clear that he had come to States to enjoy, to go places and not just spend the time in an idle manner. He was not in favour of Chander pursuing a Doctoral plan after completing his Masters. Nor was he in favour of his doing MBA. "Go for money, the almighty buck. When the going gets tough, all that matters is, how much money you have." With that note, Mohan returned to Chicago. Chander did not spend much time brooding about what his brother had advised him. At this point in time, to Chander the most important thing was to concentrate on his studies and complete his master's program in Mechanical Engineering. Then he felt, he shall be in a better position to look at it in proper perspective and plan accordingly.

Chapter XII

After Post Graduation

Year 1972 to 1980

Chander had now finished his master's program in Mechanical Engineering and was spending his time loafing around. Chander knew he had to look for a job but did not seem to be in any hurry. Los Angeles was far spread. Distances were large. Public transport was just not adequate. It plied on the main arteries only. So Chander bought himself a used car and started driving around. Now he could call and go for interviews. But when he did not have any luck, he started spending most of his time in his apartment.

Soon Chander began to feel low. He had now stopped trying to look for an employment and become lazy and lethargic. He had started sulking and preferred to stay aloof. He felt demineralised. One day, while returning from laundry room, he ran into his old friend Ash. Ash was the one who had helped Chander find a vacancy and a reference for an apartment on day one that Chander had landed in Los Angeles. Ash sensed it and said to Chander, "When I finished school (school of engineering), I made looking for a job a full-time job and in two weeks luck came to me, and I got my present job." Chander got the message. He was not going about in the right way. So from the next day, in the morning after finishing the routine three vital S's of shit, shave and shower, Chander would have a light breakfast and sit at his table with the newspaper and telephone. Chander made calls to prospective employers and did the follow up. This became his daily routine now.

In a couple of weeks, the building manager seeing a gloomy look on Chander's face gave a reference to be a Manager at a theatre- a movie hall. Chander felt that would keep him busy and also break the monotonous routine. He took the offer. The theatre had one show during weekdays and three shows on weekends. On weekdays, Chander was all alone and had to do all the work like monitoring the central air conditioning, ticketing, managing the candy counter, arranging the cash, and putting it in the locker with the statement. On Saturday and Sundays, he had two helps to manage the theatre. Upstairs, the projector room was separate and was operated by a middle-aged man, whom Chander hardly used to see. The movies used to be for children and the crowd was mostly teenagers from the local high school.

Chander had now worked for a few weeks at the theatre. Chander got an offer from a job shop company. A job shop company provided temporary job in various business establishments. Since this was an engineering job, he took it. Now, Chander had two jobs. After a couple of weeks, the long hours due to an engineering job in the day and the evening and weekends job at the cinema hall, began to be extremely tiring. The problem was solved when he got an offer to work as an engineer in a company that was to pay well. Chander quit both the jobs to take up the new job. It was in Manufacturing, it being part of Mechanical Engineering then.

Mr. Finished product was now ready to submit himself as a raw material. Chander felt very enthusiastic and was eager to learn his new job. He had educational background in the particular field and found it easy to pick up. While his seniors gave swift and clear answers to the problems that would come up, Chander found himself slow. But help was always there, and he found his colleagues very helpful and cooperative. Chander picked up fast. His supervisor liked him and took special interest in him. He introduced Chander to many tips and rules of thumb which come in handy trouble shooting on production lines. Chander became the rookie of the year.

There was an abandoned project. Cost overruns had made several engineers give up. The management decided to give it another go under Chander. Those who had worked on the project began telling Chander, what changes, modifications etc. they had made and why. They explained the problems that had arisen with respect to dimensions, breakage and repeat ability. Chander began to isolate the requirements (complaints) and the variables that had to be controlled. During the final year of his bachelor's program, he had theoretically learnt that one way to handle such a study was to control all other parameters to a constant and vary a single variable at a time. Thus you could know the individual effect of each variable and by super imposing have a sum total effect. It was then easy to know what was going on. Chander tried that as a novice, coupled with his own learning curve, a good cost had been incurred. 'Horrendous Cost' and nothing to show murmured some in the engineering department. Two days later in his bed at night, he got a brain wave. The next morning, he got ready early, got to work and waited for his chief. He discussed it and the supervisor checked the inventory in the store for a heat exchanger. A large sized was available and as requested was installed for experimental purposes. Lo and behold, it did the trick. Chander was now ready to hand over the setup to Production. The push pull technique had now been successfully applied to do nearly fifty percent ironing (deep draw) of aluminium. There were so many engineers who had worked on the setup and the enormous help many had given Chander to make it a success, the recognition of 'Citizen of Rome' a citation given to a doctor, engineer, or scientist for contributing to the advancement of knowledge in his field of endeavour, was given to Chander. He was responsible for the breakthrough. Chander had a cause to feel elated. Some of his colleagues remarked that he could now sit on his laurels for some time.

After a couple of years, Chander began to lose interest in his job. It was once in a while that a new problem came up. Mostly, it was routine. He wondered if it was two years' experience repeated several times. He got promoted to be a Senior Engineer and had now one man working for him. New responsibility got him occupied leaving no room for stray thoughts. He also got his employers sponsorship for immigration to the country.

Chander had worked for nearly six years before going for a change to a 'Power Plant Consultancy and Construction' company. Chander's prior experience was considered unrelated. Technically, it was a new line. Chander had to refresh his college studies both at undergraduate and postgraduate level. This had to be supplemented with the nuclear regulatory requirements. Interestingly since nuclear power was an emerging field, the regulatory requirements were often revised. So the concerned engineers had to stay on their toes to examine how their assigned areas and the interface with other systems was effected.

The power plant if considered one system consists of many small systems, interconnected and interdependent. This was called interface with other systems. The design and construction had evolved over decades of research and development by the industry and research institutions. CAD that is Computer Aided Design had replaced conventional design techniques. Generic designs had been created for PWR and BWR plants in various ranges. So the new approach was to take the generic design and scale it up or down as the need be to the required megawatts of power production. Chander picked up fast. The familiarisation with the relative size of equipment was essential. To a new entrant it may appear as paranoid but for obvious reasons the very essential concern with safety requirement was necessary. The balance of enthalpy for the cycle came easy because of the various courses Chander had taken while at college. Most of Chander's work consisted of sizing of pipes, pumps, heat exchangers and designing the component system as part of the whole system. With Chander's educational background, it was a challenge he enjoyed as it was new to him. Chander was assigned a couple of systems by his group leader. Chander had to have all the details of the assigned systems and the names of various systems that had interface with them on his fingertips tips. Any regulatory or other change had to be worked on in conjunction with other engineers.

A remarkable feature which had left Chander surprised because he did not appreciate when he changed his line from manufacturing to consultancy, was that as a senior engineer and with over five years of experience in the Company, he was a managerial personnel. But now in Consultancy, he was a white-collar worker. So were other engineers even though some of them were more educationally qualified. This would remain so till Chander would get to supervisory level. This called for some adjustment even though he was still living in the same neighbourhood. His status at this point in time was lower than before. But overall it was more suited to his temperament and his personality. So Chander took it in stride.

Another feature that was new to Chander was the coordination and monitoring of the construction. With communication lines a constant contact with construction was maintained. The progress at the construction site was shown in the model room on the model. The Project Engineer and the Assistant Project Engineers would monitor the progress from the model on a daily basis and occasional visits to the site. The various engineers would check the work on their systems as and when there was progress on the model. Many occasions there were phone calls from construction site which were addressed to promptly.

While the Company, itself had the contract with the utilities to have the plant designed and constructed to a specified performance, as reflected in the Design Criterion and Functional Performance, the Company contracted out to many nuclear plant equipment suppliers to have the equipment supplied. So the contract administration was an important feature. The checking of the performance of equipment at manufacturer's end before shipment to construction site was also an essential feature.

Since the Power Plant construction, is a contractual requirement from the Utility Companies coming under public inspection and scrutiny, all records including calculations for designing or sizing of equipment have to be part of public record and have to be maintained for inspection at Public Hearing. Thus the way of doing the work is different. All records are required to be documented and duly signed by concerned Registered Engineer in a standardised format and maintained in the library.

Chander's work was only in the Mechanical Engineering area. The interface and the Chemical and most importantly Nuclear area was in the separate domain. Separate teams and groups addressed themselves to these aspects. Interaction with concerned engineers of other groups was essential and fairly common.

An important safety system's study was based on simulated high energy line break. This involved assuming a high pressure and high temperature pipe bursting. The jet of fluid at high temperature and high pressure would impinge on some other pipe and cause a damage or break in the pipeline. The damage that might ensue is studied and then barriers provided. Also a pipe may break and cause two-fold damage. One the bursting jet of fluid may cause damage not only because of the failure of the system to which it belonged, and the ensuing jet may become cause of failure of some other system but also a piece of pipe may break and cause whip lash or pipe whip to the pipes in the vicinity. The model lends itself to an easy visualisation in an unlikely event of such an accident. The necessary protection cover provided to other high energy lines in the vicinity prevents further damage. Computer software programs developed to size of barriers and safety supports in the unlikely event of High Energy Line Break to avoid a catastrophic accident are used.

With seven years of experience after graduation, Chander passed the registration examination to be a 'Registered

Mechanical Engineer' in the State of California. Colloquially Chander was now a Bechtel PE.

After passing the PE exam, Chander spent a few months with his elder brother, who had now moved to Los Angeles. He lived in a bungalow facing the beach. So the weather was never very hot. The sea, as on the other beaches seemed to be quiet most of the day. At night on a clear evening, one could see some high waves. Coming from a riverbank background neither the sea nor the sea landscape fired the imagination in a manner that would have affected perhaps an Arab. The Europeans were seafaring people. Voyages and later trade ships (cargo ships) were sponsored by the kings. In India, with the littoral states, historic monuments stand as testimony to trade links with the Greek, with Rome and with the Arab nations. In the East of India, the Hindu temples and linguistic and cultural ties in the S E Asian countries speak for themselves. The great Spirit of the Chola Dynasty is not yet revived. So are the stories of the coastal States of India. How far the centralised governance has nurtured our ties dating back to ancient times and till the Muslim plunderers and subsequent assimilation from the west came, a historian will be able to do justice.

Chander was reminded of his drive six years ago, from Los Angeles to Vancouver in Canada. It was a long drive, very scenic all along the Pacific, covering the entire West Coast of America, passing through California, Oregon, and Washington and then into Vancouver, Canada. The journey was enjoyable with rest, refuelling, motels and eating places every few hours of the drive. The freeways, as they were known, (in some countries they call them expressways) were a remarkable accomplishment. One got off the freeway only if need be, otherwise, one could keep going to his destination. Chander stopped near the Boeing plant at

Seattle in Washington state, to see the plant from a distance with many planes parked. There was an observatory nearby but in the afternoon there was not much to watch. Chander stopped for a while to go up the observatory and looked through the telescope. Finally he drove to Vancouver, Canada. He drove to his friend Arun Kanti, who was a student at the University of British Columbia, at Vancouver in Canada. Chander stayed with his friend for three days. Chander's friend made his stay memorable by having a students' party at night. The next day Chander took rest. On the day before departure, Chander's friend and a couple of new friends, went in a ferry to Victoria, the capital of British Columbia. Chander drove his car straight into the ferry, where they locked his vehicle with straps on the tyres and they were free to enjoy the four-hour ride. For Chander, it was the first time that he had gone on a ferry in the sea, and he enjoyed watching the sea and dining in the ferry with friends. Indeed it was a memorable experience for Chander.

The day in Vancouver began the same way as in India, but the sun would set at nearly six in the evening. So it was still daylight at past seven in the evening. On the first evening, Chander felt different as it was already eight at night when he was thinking it to be about six. Chander supposed for the local populace it was normal and they were all accustomed to it.

Chander had another wonderful experience in Vancouver. Looking out the window at the sea Chander found the sea quiet. Out in the sea Chander saw four ships. On the second day also, he saw four ships. To Chander, it was now a part of the sea scape. Chander presumed that they were there for 'on sea repairs'. The next morning Chander woke to see only one ship. The other three had set sail at night. The distance from the room to out in the sea, where the ships had anchored, did not seem large but

Chander did not hear any engine noise. The next morning, there was no ship in sight. Apparently the last one had also left on its journey. To Chander, it was mesmerising as he felt it was time for him to leave. The university was closed for autumn break and his friend Arun suggested to him to stay on for a few more days. But somehow Chander felt he must return to Los Angeles. So he packed up and departed, heavily indebted to his friend for his hospitality and generosity. But all the same it was to remain a memorable visit to Canada.

Anyway, now he was staying at his elder brothers residence in Los Angeles. Chander's own residence was well over an hour and a half drive by freeway. While Chander was planning to return to India, his brother did not think much of it. He had worked in medical research, was an Assistant Professor, with Drew school of Medicine (under UCLA then) attached to Dr Martin Luther King hospital in Los Angeles. In a world of Publish or Perish, he had not published any paper for two years. The sponsorships he got for research were in areas not to his liking. He was playing with the idea of going into private practice. After spending nearly twelve years in the academic field and over six years at his present job, it was a big decision. The money in private practice was very inviting, nearly three to four times that in the academic world.

Since Chander's residence was at a good distance from his brothers, to meet the requirement of their parents to meet each other often, Chander sometimes would stop at his brothers place of work for a few minutes. Every time Chander drove to meet his brother he would be reminded of the great doctor Dr. Charlie's Drew, the Father of Blood Bank, who developed the technique to separate and store plasma. It was a revolution leading to large scale Blood Banks. Storage was good for a week. Platelets could be stored for five days. During the last war, the American blood could now be sent to the UK- American blood for the English as they said. Indeed it was very unfortunate, when Charles Drew had to resign in 1950 from his job with the Red Cross. Red Cross insisted that white blood be kept separate from Black Blood inspite of the fact that scientifically no difference has been established. As usual, rectification came later.

The Martin Luther King Jr. after whose name the hospital where Chander's elder brother worked, also evoked great feelings. He was a great leader. His speech,

'The March on Washington' in which he said,

"I have a dream that one day this nation will rise up and live out the true meaning of its creed."

"We hold these truths to be self-evident that all men are created equal."

To this Chander added that all persons are created equal irrespective of their race, colour, creed, province or state of origin and gender. This the theosophist believe.

Chander did not discuss these things with his elder brother. For he made his own decisions and as to where Chander's sympathies lay, he understood well. As he felt any view had to be tempered with pragmatism. It seemed that the die had already been cast. He was slowly and steadily moving towards private practice. So Chander preferred to appreciate the enormous work involved in getting started, from locating an office cum clinic in a Doctors Building to being attached to a hospital near by his own residence.

Chander wished his brother well and returned to his parents in New Delhi, India.

Epilogue

Year 1980

Chander returned to India in 1980 after practically spending the entire decade of 70's abroad. His family members and relatives told Chander in no unclear terms that the time had come for Chander to pay his debt to his father. It is an old value, no longer in vogue. It is completely out of fashion. But Chander remembered that he had made such a commitment to his father and reconciled himself to the new situation.

In the early 70's, Chander had the habit of reading the Indian newspapers at the university library in Los Angeles. That is how Chander kept himself abreast of the goings on back home in India. But by the mid-seventies Chander did not find the developments in Indian and International affairs from the Indian viewpoint of any interest to him. Instead Chander started reading the local Los Angeles newspaper. Chander recalled his short visit to India in 1977. At that time, he felt interested only in his parents, brother, sisters, and relatives. Politics, public and social matters in India were of little interest to him. Chander remembered that very well.

Now in 1980 a lot of political agitation for Khalistan and Gorkhaland was going on. While in the East the turmoil petered out soon (though DGHC was established in 1988), in the north the demand of Khalistan culminated in Operation Blue Star. It certainly quietened the matters for some time. Life became peaceful. Chander felt amused, for to him, the so-called movement had a fundamental flaw. The Sikhs talked about restoring the glory of the Panth. All very fine. The Sikhs would go back to the times of Maharaja Ranjit Singh when the Sikhs sway extended from the Frontier (now in Pakistan) in the West to Patna in the East and Maharashtra in the West and Kashmir in the North. Something like that was unimaginable in this day and age. It reminded Chander, what the crown of England had once said to Maharaja Ranjit Singh in the early part of nineteen century. "Ranjit, not all of Punjab is yours." Punjab was partitioned in 1947. Then it was reorganised in 1966 whence the state of Haryana was created and the hilly region of Solan Hills went to the new state of Himachal Pradesh. What now? Well not all the Punjabis are Sikhs. No matter how vehemently Varanasi may insist (to settle its indebtedness to the Sikhs), and the Bengalis and the Madrasis may toe the line, Maharashtra having been traditionally with the Sikhs, the fact remains, that in Punjab there are Sikhs and Monas. Unless this fact is recognised, translated into a reorganisation, the legitimate rights of all constituents are given due recognition, there cannot and shall not be any lasting peace in the region. After that is completed, the process of normalising of relations between India and Pakistan will also automatically begin. This, to Chander, was the main hurdle.

Anyway, Chander was now seeking an employment to work in his field of endeavour and settle down. Not ambitious, he was in no hurry. He began to go to the Theosophical Society lodge in the neighbourhood and talked of Universal Brotherhood of the Society, embracing all humankind irrespective of their caste, colour, creed, province or state of origin and sex. Always looking for that common thread that transcends all religions, to find the commonality and lay emphasis on that commonality. The Theosophical Society provided a platform to the people of all faiths and sects and diversity, to meet and share their thoughts. India, a plural society, had unity in diversity. This gave an opportunity to all groups of people to have a greater appreciation of one another's beliefs, aspirations and visions leading to an atmosphere conducive to have peace prevail. Chander felt that was the only way for India to preserve its rich heritage and its culture. Also it seemed to be the best way for the diverse communities to maintain their identity in an integrated India called the 'Union of India' with one flag and one national anthem.

The rapid change and advancement in technology since the last Great War has caused the humankind to come closer and discover that we are interdependent and interconnected. Events in one country are no longer viewed in isolation but as part of an occurrence of the humanity and the consequent response from the world community is inevitable. To Chander the emerging new engineering discipline of environmental engineering is a direct result of the consciousness to address ourselves to our waste and its disposal. This is essential in regard to our health, environment and for keeping our lifeline rivers clean. The climate change and call for green revolution and emissions targets are all part of the global challenges which our country is accepting to continue to be part of the world community. India is not lagging behind in its efforts to ensure a better environment for future generations. With a unified consciousness, one in mind and heart, to have a sense of one world and one humanity, the chances of success are certainly better. Chander felt that the source of inner strength lied in warm heartedness. The victory in this endeavour is victory of the humanity. This Chander was convinced of. To Chander, these and many more of the like were the new vistas, new horizons and new hopes and new challenges that he readily and wholeheartedly accepted. Chander looked forward to participating in these efforts and contribute, no matter how infinitesimally small his contribution may be.

----The End----

Acknowledgements

I express my gratitude to IGNOU for giving me the opportunity to complete the Certificate Course in Creative Writing in the year 2000. I am thankful of the faculty to give me the confidence and encouragement that I needed. Also I like to thank my class fellows, who with their friendly and sincere feelings made the learning experience enjoyable. Prof. Sanyal's personal interest in me , as he said, "I showed promise" was indeed a shot in the arm, a booster. His introducing me to the Sahitya Akademi and helping me get a library card was going out of his way to help me. Also the small close group that appeared around him of which I was a part made it all a wonderful experience.

I had earlier, some twenty or more years ago, taken up a course in Creative Writing at Cerritos in California. But due to a sudden requirement at work, I had to drop out midway. The teacher preferred to be known as teacher. I could not find out her name. Some of the students of my class would just smile at me when I tried to enquire. It was Anita Desai herself and she needed no introduction. Whatever, it left in me, a desire to complete a course in Creative Writing.

My special thanks to my better half for putting up with me during the course. My staying late to do the assignments at night after everyone went to sleep and then waking up next morning for a full day's work at office was demanding. The counselling sessions on weekends did not allow me any time for the family during the course. She took it stoically.

Why then now another twenty years later, l have started writing on my laptop. Well it was an e-mail from Som Bathla that said anyone could get started. I listened to his talk and the write up, all on my iPad and got started. Hence, this book that I conceived at Dharamshala where I had gone to attend a discourse by His Holiness the Dalai Lama on the Middling Stages of Meditation. This was soon after my mother's demise. I have been associated, since the year 2000, with Tushita Mahayana Meditation Centre, FPMT, Delhi, an organisation dedicated to preserving the Mahayana tradition of Meditation. Earlier I was a member in good standing since 1985 of Shankar Lodge of The Theosophical Society.

All the educational institutions that I have learnt from, all the organisations I have been associated with, all the places l have worked for and the numerous people who have or been a cause of my learning, have contributed, no matter how infinitesimally small, to make me what I am today. I take this opportunity to thank them all.

I presently live with my wife Anita and daughter Priya in Delhi. I thank both of them in helping me to author this book. Covid 19 has compelled people to stay indoors. Staying indoors has lead me too, to crystallise my thoughts and make this book see the light of the day.

About the Author

Jagmohan Khurana completed schooling with three different schools in New Delhi. With seventh grade being completed in Springdales Preparatory School, eighth and ninth grade in Delhi Public School, Jagmohan Khurana completed his Higher Secondary from Ramjas School, New Delhi.

A mechanical engineer by profession, he graduated from the Indian Institute of Technology, Kharagpur. Jagmohan Khurana completed his Post-Graduation from California State University at Los Angeles in California. After working as an engineer for seven years, the author passed the registration examination. Jagmohan Khurana became a registered mechanical engineer in the state of California. The author was successful in making a small contribution towards the advancement of technology. He received the Citizen of Rome Charge, which is awarded to people who contribute to advancement in the fields of science, engineering and medicine.

Jagmohan Khurana also completed a Certificate Course in Creative Writing from IGNOU.

Jagmohan Khurana lives with his wife Anita and daughter Priya in New Delhi.

INKFEATHERS PUBLISHING

India's Most Author Friendly Publishing House

Stay updated about the latest books, anthologies, events, exclusive offers, contests, product giveaways and other things that we do to support authors.

 Inkfeathers Publishing

 @InkfeathersPublishing

 @_Inkfeathers

 @Inkfeathers

 Inkfeathers.com

We'd love to connect with you!

www.ingramcontent.com/pod-product-compliance
Lightning Source LLC
LaVergne TN
LVHW040031190726
843490LV00014B/2724